TOMMY
WE HOPE YOU + YOUR PARENTS
ENJOY THIS STORY.
♡ HUGS FROM GAIL + Warren

P.S. THE AUTHOR RACHEL IS THE
DAUGHTER OF GAIL'S COLLEGE ROOM-Mate!

Flying

Henry

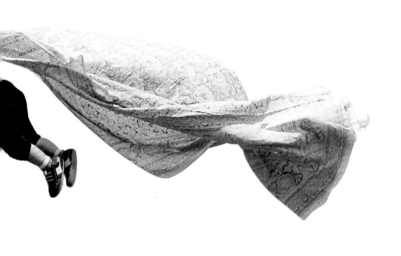

Flying Henry

by Rachel Hulin

pH **powerHouse Books** Brooklyn, NY

Henry was quite surprised when he learned he could fly.

Boy, did i

craw

Soon Henry became

c
u
r.
i
o
u
s
...

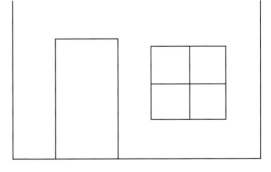

Up
he flew,
from room to room,
floating, flitting, and hovering.
Suddenly there was nothing out of his reach.

Even
bathing
became
more
fun.

Then
Henry
got

BRAVE

enough
to
fly
out
into
the
world.

He quickly
learned a few
things every
flying baby
should know:

On rainy days,
it's best to be
prepared.

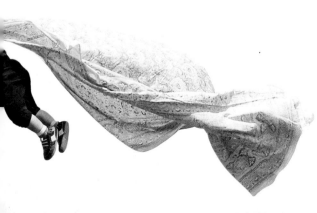

Be
friendly
to

everyone

you

meet.

Definitely

wear

a cape

for

extra

flair.

Bit by bit, Henry saw everything.

He met every animal
in the kingdom.

But
even
experienced
fliers
can
wander
into
IFFY
spaces...

and creepy places

with ghoulish faces.

Luckily,
Henry
made
a fast
escape.

"Whee!"

he
said
to
his
wagon.

And off he went.

And found a party!

The table was set, but nothing was happening yet.

Henry met a tractor,

but it wouldn't even leave the ground.

So he flew to the fair,

Henry was tired of flying alone. He decided to seek the advice of a more experienced traveler.

"Henry," said the swan

"You haven't learned the most important thing about flying."

Two flying babies

are better than one...

but it's best to fly
with a **whole flock!**

Flying Henry

© 2013 Rachel Hulin

Published in the United States by powerHouse Books,
a division of powerHouse Cultural Entertainment, Inc.

37 Main Street, Brooklyn, NY 11201-1021
T 212.604.9074 – F 212.366.5247
info@powerhousebooks.com – www.powerhousebooks.com

First edition, 2013

Library of Congress Control Number: 2012952686

ISBN: 978-1-57687-626-8

Book design by Krzysztof Poluchowicz/Alex Martin

Printed and bound in China through Asia Pacific Offset

10 9 8 7 6 5 4 3 2